The Magical Ms. Plum

The Magical Ms. Plum

Bonny Becker
illustrated by Amy Portnoy

A Yearling Book

 Published in the United States by Yearling, an imprint of Random House Children's Books, a division of Random House, Inc., New York.
Originally published in hardcover in the United States by Alfred A. Knopf, an imprint of Random House Children's Books, a division of Random House, Inc., New York, in 2009.

Yearling and the jumping horse design are registered trademarks of Random House, Inc.

Visit us on the Web! www.randomhouse.com/kids

Educators and librarians, for a variety of teaching tools, visit us at www.randomhouse.com/teachers

The Library of Congress has cataloged the hardcover edition of this work as follows:
Becker, Bonny.
The magical Ms. Plum / Bonny Becker ; illustrated by Amy Portnoy. — 1st ed.
p. cm.
Summary: The students in Ms. Plum's third-grade class soon learn that there is something very special about their teacher and her classroom's mysterious supply closet.
ISBN 978-0-375-85637-2 (trade) — ISBN 978-0-375-95637-9 (lib. bdg.) —
ISBN 978-0-375-89490-9 (e-book)
[1. Teachers—Fiction. 2. Schools—Fiction. 3. Magic—Fiction.
4. Behavior—Fiction.] I. Portnoy, Amy, ill. II. Title.
PZ7.B3814Mag 2009
[Fic]—dc22
2008042682

ISBN 978-0-375-84760-8 (pbk.)

Printed in the United States of America
10 9 8 7 6 5 4 3 2 1

First Yearling Edition 2011

Random House Children's Books supports the First Amendment and celebrates the right to read.

For Annie, who first listened
and first believed. Thank you.

Prologue

Ms. Plum had the best class in Springtime Elementary.

On a table by the window in warm, clean cages, Clyde, the hamster, skittered and chattered while a brown toad named Hip-Hop softly slumbered. They were nice animals and let everyone pet them.

On the walls hung posters that showed interesting things like the world's biggest milk shake. It was banana and filled a swimming pool! On the shelves well-loved books lay in cozy piles.

Ms. Plum's desk held a vase of plum flowers, an hourglass with plum-colored sand, and a basket. You can guess what was in the basket!

But the best thing of all about Ms. Plum's room was the supply closet. Inside, the wooden shelves sagged with colored paper, jars of crayons, bottles of glue, comic books, rulers, and rubber bands. It smelled of chalk and chocolate and something lovely no one could ever quite name.

On this particular day, the day before the first day of school, Ms. Plum stood inside this closet, talking about her new third-grade students. But who was she talking to?

"Oh, indeed," said Ms. Plum in her practical way to the paper and gum and sparkly markers. "They will be wonderful. Hopers and schemers, helpers and dreamers, jokers

and heroes. I can't wait to meet each and every one."

The crayons didn't say anything. The erasers were silent, too. School supplies make very good listeners, but they never say much back.

Even so, there were odd murmurs and rustlings from the very back of the back of the closet, where the dark was as soft as black velvet.

“Yes, of course!” exclaimed Ms. Plum. “They will be the best class ever!”

And sighing happily, she plucked up a plum-colored marker and strode briskly back into the classroom to finish getting it ready for the big day.

Chapter One

So It Begins

The next morning, the sun rose just as it should. And at 8:48 a.m., Ms. Plum stood at the front of her classroom, her hands resting neatly before her as her new students scuffled and tumbled into class.

They looked at her and quickly looked away again, not wanting to show how excited or curious (or even a little scared) they were.

Nearly every student at Springtime Elementary knew there was something about Ms. Plum's class. But the kids who had her in other years never said much. In fact, if you asked about her, funny things seemed to happen to their mouths. Their lips would open and shut, twist and turn, and finally something would pop out, like "We learned a lot about hermit crabs." But they would have this smile. A secret kind of smile, and suddenly, more than anything, you wanted to be in that class.

It was true Ms. Plum had a nice sort of tidiness about her. Her gray-blond hair sprouted up like wings behind her ears. Her plum-colored glasses, perched on her large, friendly nose, sprigged up into sparkly points. The eyes behind those glasses were a light brown color and as bright as a sparrow's. But it had to be more than her friendly look, didn't it?

Today, as the students settled into their new desks, Ms. Plum welcomed them to class and began to call roll. As the students raised their hands, Ms. Plum paused, studied each child, then wrote something on her list.

"Now then," she said, smiling with bright-eyed interest. "Who wants to get me a pencil?"

Nadia was afraid to raise her hand.

Mindy Minn was carefully arranging her things in her desk.

Why bother? thought Jeremy. Why bother with anything at all?

She should have a pencil already. Teachers are supposed to have pencils, thought Becky Oh.

Darma gnawed at the bug bites on her knuckles.

Jovi didn't understand the question.

Eric was trying to get Brad's attention.

Brad and Tashala were too busy arguing to notice anything.

Carlos raised his hand, because offering to help the teacher showed them right away that you were one of the smart ones.

But Ms. Plum pointed at Tashala and said, "Tashala, could you get me a pencil, dear?"

Tashala, looking a little startled, stopped arguing and stared at her teacher. Ms. Plum cocked her head, her sparkly glasses catching the sunlight. She nodded toward the closet.

Tashala stood up, went to the closet, opened the door, and stepped inside.

And so began another year of Ms. Plum.

Chapter Two

The Code of the West

But first, let's back up a little. About . . . three minutes should do it.

You see, Tashala Jones was going to be a cowboy. Not that she was going to be the boy part. Not that. But she intended to be rough and tough and wear spurs and chaps with no pink or purple anything.

For this first day of third grade, she wore her glossy new red cowboy boots, jeans, and a cowboy vest, so that everyone would know.

"Howdy . . . Cow-butt," whispered Brad, who was seated behind Tashala and had known her since second grade.

"Shut yer trap, E-racer Face," Tashala whispered back. And Brad did because Tashala had a mean left hook.

But soon Brad couldn't help reopening

his trap. He began to murmur more cowboy insults. Tashala hissed back racecar driver insults, because that's what Brad wanted to be, and neither noticed what Ms. Plum was saying till she pointed at Tashala and said, "Tashala, would you get me a pencil, dear?"

She nodded at the supply closet at the side of the room, and Tashala, although a little surprised, went to the closet and stepped inside.

She gazed at the jars of bright markers and fresh pink rubber bands, took a deep whiff of a strange, lovely smell (what was it?), and picked out a fat yellow pencil. Then she felt something brush against her ankle.

She looked down. A horse, no bigger than her mom's purse, swished its tail against her leg and pawed its hooves. It was chestnut-colored, with a black mane and tiny rippling muscles.

"Look what I found!" Tashala cried, bursting out of the closet.

The little horse galloped out behind her.

"How lovely, Tashala." Ms. Plum smiled and held out her hand for the pencil.

Tashala stared at Ms. Plum, then stared at the little horse. Every kid in class stared at Ms. Plum and then at the little horse. Ms. Plum didn't seem the least surprised to see a real, live horse shifting from hoof to hoof near Tashala's ankle.

Tashala handed over the pencil.

"Thank you, dear," said Ms. Plum. "Now remember, you'll have to take care of the horse."

"Sure thing," Tashala said, frowning a little behind Ms. Plum's back. She didn't like being told what to do, especially about cowboy things.

All the students looked at Ms. Plum again. And she said, "Certainly," because she knew what everyone wanted to do. The kids jumped up and clustered around Tashala and her horse.

"You're so lucky," said Mindy Minn, who had known Tashala since kindergarten. Back then Tashala had called Mindy Miss Priss and had snatched away her pink-haired Troll doll.

Of course Tashala would get a horse, thought Mindy. Tashala always knew how to get her way.

All her life Mindy had wanted a horse—a real, live horse—but the closest she got was a blue plastic pony.

"Giddy-up!" Tashala said. And to everyone's delight, he galloped around the room, his hooves rattling against the floorboards. When he got to the front of the room, he reared up for a majestic moment, pawing the air.

Everyone clapped.

"I wish I had a little horse," sighed Mindy.

Tashala snorted. "Yeah, a pink-y horsey with purple hoovies. This here's a real horse."

Tashala wouldn't even let Mindy pet the horse, because Mindy wore pink sparkly headbands and had a backpack decorated with prancing pink unicorns. Tashala hated all that pinky-pinkness. Not even a cow*girl* would have anything to do with pink unicorns.

Tashala gave the horse some water and Oaty-O cereal for chow. Then Ms. Plum told Tashala to put the stallion away in her desk. Tashala's desk was just big enough for the small horse.

Ms. Plum turned to the blackboard and wrote down their subjects for the year:

- Don't Try This at Home!
- How Many Atoms Can Dance on the Head of a Pin?
- Weird, Wonderful, Wacky Words
- What's That in Your Hair?

Tashala sat slumped down, her cowboy boots stuck out in front of her, looking as pleased as a gopher with a peanut.

Then Eric, who always had something to say, said, "P.U.! What's that?"

"No talking, please," said Ms. Plum.

But now all the kids were sniffing and making faces.

Eric pointed his nose in Tashala's direction. "It's *her,*" he announced. "Tashala stinks!"

"Do not!" said Tashala, but she was sniffing and frowning, too.

"We mustn't be rude, Eric," said Ms. Plum.

"But she smells like a barnyard," said Becky. "Can't you smell it?"

Ms. Plum sniffed carefully. "Open your desk, dear," she said.

Tashala lifted the lid. "Yuck!"

The chestnut stallion had gotten rid of his Oaty-O's the way all horses get rid of their oats. Manure lay all over the inside of Tashala's desk. There was even a big steaming pile on her new notebook with the giant silver spurs on the cover.

The horse flicked up his tail and neighed a triumphant neigh.

"Now then, you need to clean that up," said Ms. Plum.

"But it's, it's . . . poop!" protested Tashala.

"Indeed. And I think it's time for more Oaty-O's, too," said Ms. Plum.

"But then he'll . . . you know! Again!" cried Tashala.

"Well, he is a horse," said Ms. Plum sensibly.

Ms. Plum handed Tashala a brown paper bag and a little scoop.

Holding the scoop as far from herself as she could, Tashala clumsily scraped up one of the piles and dropped it into the bag. She hurriedly scooped up another pile, but it fell and landed with a juicy plop on her new cowboy boots.

"Dag nab it!" she said. Then, to everyone's surprise, she began to sniffle, wiping her nose with her sleeve.

Mindy raised her hand. "I could help Tashala clean it up, Ms. Plum."

"I'm sure Tashala would appreciate that," said Ms. Plum.

Mindy jumped up, took the scoop from Tashala, and quickly cleaned up the piles. She even cleaned off and shined Tashala's boots with a paper towel.

Tashala sniffed. "Thanks, Mindy," she whispered.

"I've changed a lot of diapers," Mindy

explained. "I have twin baby brothers. They're a couple of poop machines."

"Now, don't forget, Tashala, you'll need to muck out your desk every few hours or so," said Ms. Plum.

"Can I still help?" asked Mindy.

Tashala looked at Mindy Minn and then down at her little horse. "I think you should have him," she said.

"You do?"

Tashala straightened her shoulders. "Fair is fair. It's the cowboy code."

Mindy carefully lifted up the stallion. He seemed calm and happy in her arms. She took a deep breath of his dusty, oaty horse smell.

"Can I give him a name?" Mindy asked.

Tashala swallowed and nodded. She knew it was going to be the pinkest name ever.

And it was. But when Mindy announced that the horse was named Sir Prance-alot, Tashala squashed back her wince and gave Mindy a hearty cowboy slap on the back.

Mindy gave her such a hearty arm punch back that Tashala almost fell off her chair.

"Oh my gosh! Sorry! I have four older brothers," Mindy explained.

"No harm done," said Tashala, rubbing her arm. "You pack quite a wallop there, Mindy."

"Why, thank you," said Mindy, blushing a pretty pink.

And suddenly they both grinned.

ƍƍƍƍƍƍ

At recess, Lucy and Nadia ran up to their friend Madison.

"You won't believe what happened in Ms. Plum's class today!" Lucy said.

"It was amazing," said Nadia, her eyes wide.

And Lucy tried to say, A little horse came out of the closet. It fit in Mindy's arms!

But somehow out popped, "Horses poop!"

"So?" said Madison.

Lucy tried again. Her lips twisted and her tongue curled. She seemed to be trying really hard to say something. But out came, "Horses, they poop!"

Lucy looked at Nadia.

Nadia tried to say, It was brown with a black mane. It was real, but it wasn't scary like a real horse. It was as small as a cat.

But out came, "Horses poop a lot!"

Then she and Lucy nodded hard.

Madison stared at them like they were crazy.

Lucy looked at Nadia, and Nadia looked at Lucy. All they could do was smile. The secret smile of those who had Ms. Plum.

Chapter Three

A Parrot for Your Thoughts

Eric Soderberg had the fastest mouth in Ms. Plum's class. You had to be fast when there were eight people in your family all talking at once at the dinner table. Eric was the youngest Soderberg, so at home he barely ever got a word in edgewise.

At school it was different. Eric talked all the time and was always "stepping on other people's lines." That's what Ms. Plum called it. She said it meant that Eric was always finishing up other kids' sentences, giving their answers, and finishing their jokes.

That morning during break, Brad tried to share his new joke.

"Where do crocodiles keep their money?" he asked.

"In a riverbank," Eric said quickly.

And everyone laughed like it was Eric's joke.

Ms. Plum looked up and asked, "Who can get me some lined paper from the supply closet?"

Carlos's hand shot up first.

But Ms. Plum crooked her finger at Eric.

Carlos started to say, "Hey, that's—"

"Not fair," Eric finished for him. "Sorry, dude."

Eric grinned and went to the supply closet. He opened the door and stepped inside. He took a deep whiff of the yummy, nameless smell and picked out five sheets of lined paper. Next to the stack of paper he saw a little green parrot staring at him. The parrot had bright black eyes and a red spot on his head. Was he real? The parrot cocked his head left, and then right. He was real!

"Wow!" said Eric. "That's so—"

"Awesome!" squawked the parrot.

Then the parrot fluttered up to roost right on top of Eric's head. Eric could feel the claws digging into his scalp.

"Don't bite!" squawked the parrot.

That's just what I was thinking, thought Eric, but even so, having a talking parrot was worth the risk.

"Look what I found!" cried the parrot as Eric hurried from the closet.

Eric had been just about to say that very same thing.

"Cool!" said the kids.

Ms. Plum smiled cheerfully, took the lined paper from Eric, and nodded for him to sit down.

Eric caught a glimpse of himself in the mirror at the back of the room. The parrot on his head made him look like a pirate.

"Ahoy, mateys!" screeched the parrot. For such a little bird, he was awfully loud.

"We will now review some important facts and statistics," said Ms. Plum.

The class sat up straighter. Ms. Plum's important facts and statistics weren't like anybody else's.

"How many people in the world have the same birthday as you?" she asked.

Eric raised his hand. He always had his hand up to answer class questions, even when he wasn't really paying attention. But before he could make up an answer, the parrot squawked, "I can see Becky's underwear!"

Becky glared at Eric.

"The parrot said it," cried the parrot.

"But you thought it, didn't you?" said Brad.

But before Eric, or his parrot, could answer, Ms. Plum called them back to attention and asked, "Well, who can tell me how a jar of peanut butter can make you rich?"

Eric raised his hand again.

"Mindy smells pretty," said the parrot with a parroty sigh.

The class started to giggle.

"Shut up!" said the parrot. "Not you," said the parrot as Eric gestured wildly to the class. "Him!" said the parrot as Eric pointed an accusatory finger at the bird.

Eric tried to make his mind go blank.

"I'm thinking nothing, nothing, nothing," murmured the parrot.

"What else is new?" said Brad, and the class cracked up again.

"That's not funny!" cried the parrot. "I tell better jokes than you."

"You mean you *steal* better jokes," said Brad.

"Geez, I really have to go to the bathroom," said the parrot. "I wish I hadn't eaten those beans last night."

The class roared as Eric reached up and tried to grab his beak. The parrot scrambled out of reach, his claws digging like pins into Eric's scalp.

"Ms. Plum! Help me! How do I get rid of him?" the parrot squawked.

Ms. Plum said, "I'm sure you'll think of something, Eric. You're a smart boy."

Eric glanced up at the parrot, who was now preening his feathers in a smug sort of way, and Eric's eyes got a kind of gleam. The parrot began to murmur softly, dreamily. "Nice birdie. Birdie go away. Far, far away. Back into the closet, okay?"

Eric gave Ms. Plum a questioning look. Ms. Plum nodded, and he slipped from his desk and walked toward the closet.

"Here you go," crooned the parrot. "Back in the nice warm closet. Birdie bye-bye."

Everyone could still hear him murmuring as Eric slipped inside the closet and then burst out again, slamming the door shut behind him. The parrot was gone from his head.

Eric opened his mouth, hesitated, then said softly, "Is he gone?"

Everyone listened carefully. No sound from the closet.

"Why don't you check?" said Tashala. "Look in the closet."

But Eric shook his head. "That's okay," he said, and he slipped back to his desk.

There on his desk was a yellow sheet of paper. How had that gotten there? No one else had one. Eric picked up the flyer. It said something that made Eric grin. He looked at Ms. Plum. But Ms. Plum was writing out a new fact on the board.

"Did Ms. Plum put this on my desk?" Eric asked.

Tashala stared at him. "When could she have done that?"

Eric didn't know, but he neatly folded the flyer and stuck it in his pocket.

And at recess, when Brad said, "What's a

polygon?" Eric knew the answer to that, but he let Brad say it.

Q: How many people in the world have the same birthday as you?
A: About twenty million.

Q: How can a jar of peanut butter make you rich?
A: Turn it into diamonds! All you need is to cook the peanut butter at a temperature of 3,000 degrees under pressure of over a million pounds per square inch.

Q: What did the flyer say?
A: "Good with words? Come join the Springtime Elementary Debate Team. First meeting today after school!"

Q: What's a polygon?
A: A missing parrot!

Chapter Four

At Your Service

Being the smartest kid in the class, Carlos had figured out that the animal you found in the closet could kind of turn out to be a problem if *you* had a problem—like being a cowboy snob like Tashala or an interrupter like Eric.

But Carlos couldn't think of any problem with being smart. He couldn't wait to get picked and to find out what his animal would be. He figured it would be something super clever.

Today Ms. Plum was showing them how to tie a turban.

"First you put the end of the cloth in your moush," she said, biting onto the end of the long piece of orange cloth. "Then you wap it around—"

Then Ms. Plum sniffled and asked, "Who cansh get me some Kleenex?"

Carlos's hand shot up. But Ms. Plum picked . . . Darma! Darma, who hadn't even raised her hand. Who never raised her hand! She was almost as quiet as Jovi, who was from Africa and didn't speak English very well.

Darma was so messy and clumsy. She was always getting glue in her hair or mud on her shoes and bug bites on her hands that she scratched until they were scabby.

But Ms. Plum looked right past Carlos's waving, wriggling hand and nodded at her. "Darma, could you, pleash?"

Darma blushed so hard she had tears in her eyes. She stood up hesitantly and knocked over her chair. "Sorry," she said, quickly setting the chair back up and patting it. Then she tripped on her shoe strap. "Sorry," she mumbled. At last Darma made it to the closet.

She was gone a long time. Ms. Plum continued with her lesson on turban wrapping, and it was really hard to pay attention. Although everyone wanted to wear a turban, as Ms. Plum had promised they could, they kept wondering what was taking Darma so long.

Finally Darma poked her head out and said, "I can't find the Kleenex." Then she looked down and said, "Oh."

A squad of bright-eyed squirrels strode from the closet, walking on their hind legs, carrying the Kleenex box above their heads like a bunch of servants carrying Cleopatra on her throne. They marched the Kleenex over to Ms. Plum's desk.

Ms. Plum put the final tuck into her turban and looked down at the squirrels.

"Why, thank you, squirrels!" she said, giving Darma a kindly look. "Very nice, dear. Very nice, indeed."

Darma didn't quite know what Ms. Plum was talking about, but still it made her feel good.

The squirrels scurried to Darma's desk, apparently to await further orders.

Darma stumbled back to her chair.

She placed her hands neatly in front of her to show that she was listening to Ms. Plum and to get the other kids to stop staring. The squirrels took one look at her ragged fingernails, disappeared into the closet with flicks of their tails, and reemerged with nail clippers, a nail file, and a bottle of soft pink nail polish.

While Ms. Plum strode about the room in her turban, telling them about India, Darma got a lovely manicure.

"Hey, can I get one of those?" Mindy whispered across the aisle.

Mindy had never said anything to Darma before.

Darma tried shooing the squirrels in Mindy's direction, but they just perched on the edge of Darma's desk, their bright eyes shining on her. Eager smiles on their faces. Their tails at attention.

Darma took the bottle of nail polish and set it next to Mindy. One of the squirrels leapt onto Mindy's desk and whisked the bottle of polish away.

"Yipes!" cried Mindy.

"Sorry," said Darma, nervously picking at her new manicure.

The squirrels marched back to the closet with the manicure stuff. After a moment they came out with assorted candies, including a giant bag of chocolate Kisses. They hauled it all over to Darma.

"You have to share those," said Becky Oh.

"Sorry," said Darma. She tried passing out Kisses to the class, but the squirrels grabbed them and scurried every one back to her. The Kisses sat in a big foil-wrapped pile in front of her.

The squirrels stared at her expectantly. One of them held up a Kiss for her in its little paw. When she didn't take it, they all bent their heads, drooped their tails, and looked horribly sad.

For the first time ever, Darma raised her hand.

"Yes, Darma?" said Ms. Plum.

"Is it okay if I eat a candy?" she asked, nodding at the sorrowful squirrels.

"Certainly, dear," said Ms. Plum. "I think it would be the kind thing to do."

So Darma ate one Kiss. The squirrels still looked sad. She ate two. The squirrels still looked sad. Darma had to eat fifteen chocolate Kisses, five caramels, and a bag of M&M's before they began beaming again.

"Sorry," Darma kept saying with each bite. "Sorry." She gave a little burp.

Then the squirrels really got serious. They organized Darma's binder. They buffed her shoes with their tails. They combed her hair with their cunning little paws. They sharpened her pencils. They couldn't do enough for her.

"How come she gets all this cool stuff done for her?" complained Becky Oh.

Ms. Plum looked thoughtful. "Maybe our Darma is cool," she finally said.

The kids all stared at Darma. Miss Scabby Bug Bites was cool?

Darma shrugged sheepishly and kept saying "Sorry." But she didn't look *that* sorry. In fact, she looked quite pleased at the way the squirrels had arranged her hair.

When Darma had to leave after school, the squirrels clung to her ankles and made pitiful whining sounds. One tried desperately to polish her shoes even as she stepped out the door.

"Thank you so much," she said, turning back. The squirrels stood in a line at the door. "But I really have to get home."

The squirrels all gave a tremendous mutual sigh.

The next morning, the squirrels were gone, but they had tidied up Darma's desk, spell-checked her essay on the Taj Mahal, and left a pile of pink bubble gum.

"You're so lucky," gushed Emiko.

"I wish I had a bunch of squirrel helpers," said Becky Oh.

"Want some gum?" said Darma shyly.

The girls nodded.

"Me too?" asked Mindy.

Darma handed them each a piece of gum.

"I like your new shirt," said Mindy.

"I made it myself," said Darma.

"I wish I could sew," said Mindy.

"Well, one sleeve is kind of on backward. . . ."

"Oh, I thought that was a cool new style. Pink's my favorite color," Mindy added, snapping her gum. "What's yours?"

"Blue," said Darma, blushing and pointing the toes of her almost shiny shoes.

Then she looked up at Ms. Plum and smiled like the sun.

QQQQQQ

Carlos thought that if he could just figure out the rules, he could get chosen for the supply closet. So the night after Darma got her squirrels, Carlos wrote down what he knew so far.

Animals came only from the closet.

No one was able to talk about the animals outside Ms. Plum's room.

The animals couldn't leave the classroom. (He was pretty sure.)

The animals disappeared by the next day. (Sir Prance-alot had been gone the next morning, and so had the squirrels.)

It helped if you were pathetic or a loudmouth or had some kind of problem.

This was the most important rule. And that obviously was the trouble. Carlos needed to be much less amazing and wonderful than he was!

So the next day, Carlos started throwing eraser bits at the back of Brad's neck. It took Brad a while to figure out what was happening. But when he did, he glared at

Carlos so hard that Carlos began to worry about what might happen at recess.

Besides, he started to wonder what kind of animal a class pest would find. Probably a giant cockroach.

He figured, if you wanted a good animal, it was better to be someone people felt sorry for, like Darma. Well, like Darma used to be.

The next morning, Carlos wore his old pants from second grade. They were too short and had holes at the knees.

"Hey, your baby brother called. He wants his pants back!" said Brad.

"Where's the flood, Hi-Pants?" said Becky Oh.

She and Brad high-fived each other.

Just as he had hoped—kids were being mean to him!

When Carlos sat down, he could barely breathe, his pants were so tight. By lunchtime his legs were numb. It was really uncomfortable pretending to be poor and sad. And Ms. Plum never even noticed how pitiful he was, anyway.

Then he remembered Mindy. She had done a good deed and gotten that neat horse.

Carlos did good deeds all the following day. He picked up dropped pencils, opened doors, and let Eric cut in front of him in line at lunch. He even tried to get Jeremy to laugh by telling him a joke, but Jeremy just stared at him.

Still, it was the thought that counted, right? Carlos looked hopefully at Ms. Plum.

She smiled warmly at him, but that was all. No one was asked to go to the closet that day or for the next two weeks, long after Carlos had become tired of doing good deeds.

So now he knew Rule 6. You couldn't predict when or why or what would happen with the closet. All he could do now was wait and wait and wait. . . .

Then Carlos had an awful thought. What if Ms. Plum never picked him? No, that wasn't possible . . . was it?

Chapter Five

Fly Away Home

Jovi didn't speak English very well. Ms. Plum explained to them how Jovi had escaped with his family from a place in Africa where bad things had happened. Jovi had gentle brown eyes and a soft smile, like he wished he could say yes to everything.

Jovi never raised his hand for the supply closet, but even so, one bright fall day Ms. Plum called on him.

Ms. Plum was showing them the basics of classical fencing.

"Jovi," she suddenly said.

And when he looked up from his homemade sword—a cardboard tube taped to a wooden handle—she held up an empty roll of tape, smiled, and nodded toward the supply closet.

Jovi smiled back and quickly went to the closet.

Back in the third row, Carlos slumped over his "sword." He had never lived where really bad things had happened.

"Now watch carefully," Ms. Plum said. "This is the en garde position. The position you take just before the fencing match begins."

Jovi quickly came back with the tape. A bird streaked out of the closet behind him. It perched on a narrow pipe that ran just below the ceiling. It was a golden falcon with a beak that curved into a sharp point.

The falcon glared down at the classroom with glittering eyes.

"Awesome!" said Brad. "He's not like a horse or a parrot or those squirrels. He's a real wild animal."

Brad was right. You could tell by the falcon's fierce yellow eyes. And the way it jolted its head around, fast and sure and wary.

Nadia sucked her lip. The falcon looked like it would bite.

"Now, the key is to hold your sword lightly but with confidence," Ms. Plum said, continuing with her lesson.

But Tashala couldn't help herself. She

dropped her cardboard tube and took a piece of beef jerky out of her desk and held it up toward the falcon.

The falcon blinked. With a sudden high screech, the bird of prey launched itself from the pipe, swooped down on Tashala, and snatched the jerky in its claws. Tashala could feel the breeze from its wings. It flew back to the pipe and tore into the meat.

"Wow!" said Tashala.

Ms. Plum didn't scold. In fact, she cocked her head, her brown eyes bright, as if Tashala and the bird were an interesting experiment.

With that, most everyone rushed to get food from their lunches and hold it up for the falcon—potato chips, a Twinkie, a pickle.

"Falcons don't eat pickles," said Becky Oh.

But Mindy ignored her and waggled the green slice toward the bird.

Jovi stood near the back of the room and smiled timidly.

At first when the falcon grabbed some food, it was cool. But then the bird kept swooping down on people, even when no one wanted it to anymore. Sometimes it would dive-bomb a kid's head for no reason. Lucy was sure the bird would bury its pointed beak in the back of her neck.

Pretty soon the students of Ms. Plum's class had their necks hunched into their

shoulders or were cringing under their desks.

"We gotta get it back into the closet!" cried Eric as the bird jetted over his desk, screeching and scattering his papers.

No one asked Jovi what to do with his bird.

Eric tried flapping his jacket at it and shooing it toward the closet, but the falcon just yawned, showing a tiny black tongue.

Carlos stood right in front of the open closet door, waving some bologna.

"Look, food!" he cried.

For a minute it looked like Carlos's idea would work. The falcon swooped toward him, but at the last second, the bird banked, grabbed the bologna in its claws, and zoomed back to its perch on the pipe.

Becky grabbed her cardboard tube and heaved it at the bird. "Go back where you belong, Feather-butt!"

"That won't work," said Brad. He picked up an eraser and threw it hard. He almost hit the falcon, who didn't seem to understand that some people were throwing things at it.

And that's when a voice from the back of the room said, "No."

It took a moment for everyone to realize that it was Jovi.

Jovi's shoulders were tight points under his shirt. It seemed like it made him nervous to have everyone look at him and to not say yes, but even so, he said, a second time, "No. No hurting."

Some of the kids remembered that in a way, the falcon belonged to Jovi. Others remembered, too, about the bad things Jovi's gentle eyes had seen.

"It's not his fault he doesn't want to go back into the closet," Tashala admitted.

"Well, then what are we gonna do?" asked Brad.

Jovi jerked his chin toward the window. For a second he looked almost like a falcon himself, with his fine, sharp nose and the determined look in his dark eyes.

"Free," he said.

They all looked at Ms. Plum.

She nodded.

"But I thought the animals couldn't leave the room," said Carlos.

"Each animal can choose for itself," said Ms. Plum; she didn't explain any further.

Tashala pulled down the top of one of the windows.

Amazingly, the falcon flew down from the pipe and perched on Jovi's forearm. Jovi's arm shook, but he carried the bird over to the window.

"Fly away now," said Jovi. "Freedom for you."

"Say, you're really learning your English," said Carlos.

Jovi straightened his shoulders. His dark eyes shone.

"I am being good with English," he said proudly.

"You really are," said Carlos.

"Screeeeeeeee," cried the falcon. Then it flapped its wings and flew out into the high blue sky.

Chapter Six
Woe Is Me

The gloomiest kid in Ms. Plum's room was Jeremy. Jeremy's favorite word was *doom*. His favorite weather was wet. His favorite color was black.

Jeremy always wore black shoes, black socks, black pants, and a black T-shirt. When he grew up, he wanted a tattoo of a cobweb on his arm.

Jeremy never smiled because, he said, "It's a weary, weary way."

No one knew quite what that meant, but it was the sort of thing Jeremy liked to say.

"Who can get me a glue stick?" asked Ms. Plum one rainy October afternoon.

Jeremy slowly raised his hand, propping it with his other hand and letting his fingers hang pale and limp.

When Ms. Plum picked him, he walked in a weary, weary way to the closet.

Carlos let out a big, weary sigh, glanced at Ms. Plum, but knew it was pointless. He could come into class in a coffin and it wouldn't make Ms. Plum pick him.

A moment later Jeremy stepped out of the closet with a small raven hunched on his shoulder. It was dark black, with black eyes and a black beak that looked too heavy for its head.

"Nevermore," Jeremy said in a grimly satisfied way. "Nevermore."

"Huh?" said Lucy.

Ms. Plum explained that Jeremy was referring to a famous poem by Edgar Allan Poe about a raven who only said "nevermore" to everything.

"'Quoth the raven,'" said Jeremy with a faint nod of his head. "'Nevermore.'"

"Quoth?" asked Eric.

"Means 'said,'" explained Carlos.

Jeremy slumped back to his seat, noticing with satisfaction in the mirror how the bird crouched on his shoulder, looking as gloomy as midnight.

"Maybe your raven will say something," said Eric.

"Beware," said Jeremy, "for they are messengers of death."

Nadia bit her lip.

Eric grinned and said, "Awesome!"

"Speak, dark one," said Jeremy. "Tell them of their doom."

"Pig snout," said the raven.

"Pig snout? What's that mean?" said Darma.

Jeremy frowned.

"Speak to us of bleakness," commanded Jeremy. "Speak of sorrow."

"Pig snout," said the raven.

Darma and Mindy giggled.

Jeremy couldn't believe it. "That's not what ravens say," he complained.

The raven hunched its dark shoulders. It looked very gloomy and woeful on Jeremy's shoulder, but no matter what Jeremy did or said, all it would croak was "Pig snout."

Jeremy spent the whole morning with "pig snout" in his ear. The other students came over at break time and asked the bird questions just to hear it say "Pig snout."

"What's fifteen times three?" asked Eric.

"Pig snout."

"What's the capital of Japan?" asked Emiko.

"Pig snout."

"Would you like a knuckle sandwich?" said Brad.

"Pig snout."

But they needn't have bothered. The raven was happy to say "Pig snout" anytime. Just at random, in the middle of nothing, he would say "Pig snout."

He said it loudly. He said it softly. He murmured it. He squawked it in a sharp croak.

"Stop saying that!" Jeremy finally said.

"Pig snout," whispered the raven in his ear.

"You stink," said Jeremy.

"Piiiiggg snouuuut," crooned the raven.

"You're a big phony!"

"P-p-p-p-pig snout," the raven rapped out.

"Why, I oughta—"

"Pigsnoutpigsnoutpigsnout," the raven said really, really fast.

And then it happened . . . Jeremy started to giggle.

He squished his hands over his mouth, but he couldn't stop. First the giggle was like a tiny bubble of air escaping from the side of his mouth. Then it was like a rippling stream. Then it was a laugh—a laugh so loud and hard that Jeremy buried his head in his arms, his chest shaking.

The raven complained with a loud "Pig snout!" And glared.

But Jeremy just kept laughing until it seemed every laugh he'd ever had inside was laughed out of him. Finally he raised his head from his arms, wiped the tears off his cheeks, and shook his head happily.

"Man, oh, man," he said, smiling at Ms. Plum. "Pig snout?"

"Indeed," said Ms. Plum with a smile.

And then she told him it was time for the raven to go back.

"Pig snout," Jeremy said, closing the closet door with a little salute and a lopsided grin.

And the next day, Jeremy came to school in bright red high-tops and a tie-dyed T-shirt bursting with lemon yellow stars.

ƍƍƍƍƍƍ

One December afternoon Ms. Plum walked over to the closet and opened the door. She didn't go inside. Instead she held up one of her plums and called out, "Sweets for my sweets."

Soon there was a sound of faraway voices and a faint creaking from the closet. The sound grew closer. Every eye was on the closet doorway.

Suddenly a band of miniature monkeys came striding forth, chittering and screaming. Half a dozen of the monkeys pulled a wagon filled to the brim with candy.

The little monkeys grabbed the candies and raced around the room giving them to the students. They weren't like any candy the kids had ever had.

Tashala got a pink and white candy shaped like a rabbit. When she bit into it, it exploded like a cloud of cotton candy in her mouth, filling it with the taste of strawberries and cream.

Jeremy got a candy that looked like a zebra lollipop. When he stuck it in his mouth, he realized that each stripe had a different flavor.

"It's chocolate. Hmmmm, no—

butterscotch. Licorice! I don't know what that one is, but it's good!"

Carlos got a handful of tiny gumballs. At least they looked like gumballs—but a monkey grabbed one and heaved it at the ground, and it bounced around the room like a Super Ball. Then the monkey opened its mouth and the gumball landed inside. Score!

Carlos quickly tossed one of the balls. It caromed off the floor, the ceiling, a light fixture, Mindy's desk, and when he opened his mouth, it hit his tongue and instantly dissolved into a taste of sweet lemonade with maybe just a bit of dust.

Every student got a different candy, and later, thinking about it, everyone felt they had gotten exactly the right candy for them.

As soon as the monkeys had given out their candy, they scampered onto Ms. Plum's desk and eagerly took several plums from her basket. They piled them in the wagon and pulled it back into the closet. The door shut slowly behind them.

"Why did we get the candy?" asked Tashala.

"Because," said Ms. Plum.

"Because we all did good on our spelling tests?" asked Becky Oh.

"Because it's Friday?" asked Brad.

"Because it's almost Christmas?" asked Nadia.

"No," said Ms. Plum. "Just because."

"Why did the monkeys get your plums?" asked Lucy.

"Because they gave us candy?" asked Eric.

"Because they were cute?" asked Emiko.

"Because they go ape for your plums?" asked Jeremy. "Get it?" He snortled at his own joke. "Go ape?"

"Just because," said Ms. Plum.

"Just because of what?" said Carlos. He didn't like not knowing the exact answer to things.

Ms. Plum surveyed the class. Her students were finishing up their treats, licking their fingers and lips, and smiling happy smiles. She tilted her head. In the winter sunlight, the tips of her glasses sparkled like purple frost. She happily licked the plum lollipop the monkeys had given her.

"Just because," she finally said to Carlos. "Sometimes, the answer is just because."

ʘʘʘʘʘʘ

Chapter Seven
All Aboard

Outside the windows of Ms. Plum's classroom, the snow fell in easy swirls.

"Like popcorn," wrote Eric.

"Like feathers," wrote Darma, working on the snow poem Ms. Plum had assigned.

"Like happiness," wrote Emiko.

"Like . . ." But Brad couldn't think of what the snow was like except like snow.

He stared out the window and pretended to be thinking about his poem, but what he was really thinking about was the big snowball fight at recess.

The students weren't supposed to have snowball fights, but the playground fell in a long slope toward the back parking lot. The teachers huddled by the warmth of the lunchroom doors, and most couldn't see below the slope.

These fights usually involved fifth-grade

boys, but Brad had joined in anyway. They put up with him because they could pelt him and he'd keep coming back. Brad was tough. "Like a Mack truck," Brad's dad said. Brad didn't know exactly what a Mack truck was, but to be like a truck was really good, as far as Brad was concerned.

Out of all of Ms. Plum's students, Brad was the only one who wasn't sure he even wanted to get a closet animal.

The animals seemed kind of babyish—squirrels who did manicures, a talking parrot who didn't really talk like a pirate, a pooping pony. The falcon had been cool and the raven made him laugh, but the falcon flew away and Brad sure didn't need help laughing in class.

The monkeys had been the best, for sure. And to his surprise, when he turned back to his snow poem, he noticed one of them creeping out from the closet door.

Brad quickly looked around. Had anyone else noticed? All the other kids were working on their poems. Ms. Plum was staring out at the snow with a dreamy look.

The little monkey glanced around, its eyes bright with curiosity. Brad carefully lowered his hand by his desk and waggled his pencil with his fingers. He soon felt the monkey's paws on his hand, grabbing for the pencil.

Brad scooped him up and gently slipped the monkey into the pocket of his hooded sweatshirt.

Glancing down, he saw that the monkey had positioned itself so it could peer out of his pocket. He seemed quite content.

I'm going to call him Chompers, Brad thought. Since no one else knows about him, maybe I could keep him.

Could he take the monkey out of the classroom? Ms. Plum said the animals made their own choice. The little monkey had sneaked out of the closet. He must want to be free, Brad decided.

Brrinng!

The buzz of the recess bell cut into his thoughts.

He shrugged on his parka, carefully transferring Chompers to his coat pocket, and joined the line heading out of the classroom. Step one. There was Ms. Plum's smiling face. Step two. There was the open door. Step three. He was out!

He slipped his hand into his pocket, and Chompers immediately jumped on it and scrambled up his arm to perch on his shoulder.

Could anyone else see him? The other kids in Ms. Plum's classroom had scattered like . . . like what? Brad couldn't think of how they'd scattered except like a bunch of kids at recess.

Brad raced for the back slope of the playground. He'd done it! He had his very own monkey!

"Look what I got!" shouted Brad, coming over the slope, skidding, and almost falling in the snow.

Chompers chattered excitedly and grabbed Brad's ear to hang on.

This would be like the most amazing thing the fifth-grade boys had ever seen.

Only they couldn't see it.

"What?" said Michael. "A new hat? Big deal."

"Run!" shouted Ron, heaving a snowball at Brad and almost hitting Chompers.

"Hey, watch it!"

No one ever wanted to challenge Ron. He was the number one pitcher on the baseball team and led Ultimate Frisbee, too.

Even so, Brad crushed some snow into a ball and heaved it at Ron. Just as the snowball left his hand, Chompers leapt onto it.

Brad stared, his mouth slack, as his monkey rode the snowball right smack into Ron's chest. Then Chompers was coming back toward him atop Ron's snowball—coming straight at Brad's face. But just before the snowball reached him, the monkey pushed off, sending the snowball harmlessly to Brad's left and launching himself back onto Brad's shoulder.

Chompers was chattering with joy. His eyes wild, his fur blown up like he'd touched a light socket.

So Brad, dodging snowballs, quickly scooped up another snowball and sent it flying.

Chompers rode with it. Amazingly, he even rose to his feet like a surfer on a surfboard.

And suddenly Brad could feel just what the monkey was feeling. He could feel the icy, crusty ball of snow wobbling under his toes. He could feel the wind whipping at his cheeks. He could feel how Chompers leaned this way and that, steering the snowball right into Ron's face!

Bull's-eye!

Ron clawed off the snow, revenge in his eyes. Brad started backpedaling as fast as he could. Ron rocketed a snowball straight at him.

But Brad knew that the monkey would push it away and Ron's best throw would never hit him.

Now Ron was furious, and he waved away the other boys. This was just between him and Brad.

Five throws and it was over.

Throw number one: Brad to Ron. Result: A face full of snow for Ron.

Throw number two: Ron to Brad. A perfect missile of packed snow that at the last second swerved over Brad's shoulder.

Throw number three: Brad to Ron. A high throw that looked like it would miss by a mile but instead veered this way and that (was there a wind up there?) and splatted onto Ron's astonished face. Result: A lot of fifth-grade boys laughing their heads off.

Throw number four: Ron to Brad. Another missile. A heat-seeking missile. A Brad-seeking missile. A sizzling fastball that seemed to gradually slow, landing softly about three feet from Brad and then rolling to a stop at his feet.

Throw number five: Brad to Ron. A good, hard throw. And no matter how much Ron ducked and dodged, the thing seemed to follow. And for the fourth time Ron had to wipe cold, wet snow from his eyes.

Ron turned and walked up the playground slope.

"I'm done," he said.

The rest of the fifth-grade boys clustered around Brad, walking with him back to the upper play yard, laughing and yelling about the best snowball fight in history.

"You turning out for baseball this spring?" asked Michael.

"Maybe," said Brad, who hadn't been planning on it. But now, with Chompers on his side, anything was possible.

It had probably been the best day of his life, Brad decided on the bus ride home.

He'd been a little worried that Chompers might disappear back into the closet after recess. Then he'd been worried that Chompers would disappear once he left the school grounds. But there he was in Brad's coat pocket. He did seem a little sleepy, but who wouldn't be after vrooming around on an icy snowball.

Brad hung out in his room with Chompers for the rest of the afternoon. But a little worm of worry began to curl and twist in his stomach. Chompers wasn't looking so good. His bright eyes had become dull. He sat on Brad's desk, staring at the falling snow.

Brad tried to feed him a banana, but Chompers wasn't interested. He tried cheese, almonds, an Oreo. Chompers wouldn't even try a taste.

"Don't you want to stay, Chompers? Don't you like it here?" Brad asked.

He stroked the tiny monkey's back. "We could have so much fun," Brad said. "Snowballs are nothing. Wait till you ride a Frisbee! And that supply closet is all dark. I mean it's not like outside."

Chompers sighed.

Brad swallowed.

And suddenly he had that feeling again, like he was Chompers. He felt like he was in the closet with his brothers and sisters, chattering and shrieking. Happy and excited.

"You're the coolest thing that ever happened to me," Brad whispered, pushing back something that might have been tears.

The next morning, he hurried into class as soon as the bus arrived at school. He took Chompers from his pocket, opened the closet door, crouched down, and set him inside. Chompers immediately perked up. His eyes snapped with life; his fur glowed.

"Goodbye, Chompers," Brad said quickly, before the little monkey disappeared.

Chompers turned and stared at him for a moment. Then he gave a big monkey grin and started to scramble up the shelves toward the sound of other monkey voices.

Brad suddenly knew that up there, back behind the markers and paper and glue, was a big place of open sky, green trees, and soft, warm breezes that felt like . . . that felt like home.

"Are you okay, Brad?"

Brad jumped. There behind him stood Ms. Plum.

"I—I lost something," Brad said, standing up. "I was looking for it."

"Here, I'll help you," said Ms. Plum, kneeling on the floor.

"Well, actually—" Brad started to say.

Ms. Plum stood back up, holding a brochure. "Here, perhaps this is what you need?"

Brad stared at the blue and white brochure. He hadn't seen anything on the floor before. Then he saw the picture on the front: a guy launched into the air against a bright blue sky. It looked a lot like Chompers on a snowball.

Brad glanced at Ms. Plum. Did she know?

Underneath the picture were the words "Mad Monkee Snowboarding Lessons. Ever wanted to snowboard? Now's your chance!"

Inside was information about costs and times and equipment.

Brad folded the brochure and stuck it in his pocket. He'd ask his dad about lessons tonight.

Brad looked at Ms. Plum again. She was busy marking some folders.

She knows, thought Brad.

And he said "Thanks" to no one in particular as he headed back out to the playground.

He ran for the slope to the parking lot and skidded down it. A couple of fifth graders were heaving snowballs, but Brad turned and climbed back up the hill. Skidded down it again, waving his arms for balance, trying to hold his feet close together.

Up and down, up and down, up and down—Brad practiced until the bell called him in to class.

On the bus, Carlos pretended to be reading his book, but really he was listening to Jeremy behind him, making jokes. Jeremy was like the funniest kid in school now.

Carlos grumpily propped his cheek against his fist. Everyone was getting something cool from the supply closet but him. Darma still got glue in her hair, but she and Mindy and Tashala were best friends. Eric was learning how to debate. Jovi stood taller and spoke louder in class.

It wasn't fair. He did everything right. He was the best student. He was nice . . . mostly. He raised his hand the fastest, every time!

Ms. Plum just didn't like him. She liked all the other kids, but not him.

". . . to get to the other side!" Jeremy said, finishing his joke. And the kids around him burst into laughter.

Carlos didn't laugh. He bent closer over his book and scowled.

They all thought they were so smart. He'd show them.

The next day at recess, he waited till everyone left the classroom. When he was sure he was alone, Carlos sneaked a look in Darma's desk. There was a nice pile of pink bubble gum. He took one.

Then he peeked in Mindy's desk. There was a note.

"Eric likes you! I just know it!" It was signed by Lucy.

When Darma and Mindy came in from recess, he was afraid they would somehow know that he had snooped. But they didn't.

So, when no one else was around, Carlos

started peeking in other kids' desks and going through the pockets of their coats and looking in their book bags. Lucy had a note from her mom saying she needed to go to the doctor for a rash. Tashala had a picture of a horse in her desk, with horse names written all over it. Eric had Brad's Game Boy, even though Carlos knew he'd told Brad that he'd left it at his house.

Carlos never tattled on anybody, but he liked looking at the other kids' stuff and knowing things that they didn't know he knew. He felt smarter than ever.

ꝏꝏꝏ

Chapter Eight

Rose-Colored Glasses

Emiko looked a little like Hip-Hop, the toad. She was squat and sturdy and wore thick glasses that made her eyes look bulgy. But even though some kids teased her, she was always smiling, because whatever you said, she took it as a compliment.

"Your eyes look like a frog's," Becky Oh said, feeling mean one day early in the school year.

"Thank you!" said Emiko. "Frog eyes are so sparkly."

Everything was good for Emiko.

A freezing cold day was as fun as a sno-cone.

A dark, damp day smelled cozy.

A bad grade on a paper was marked in a pretty red.

Ms. Plum said Emiko saw the world through rose-colored glasses.

"Her glasses look regular-colored to me," said Tashala.

"It means she sees everything like it's better than it really is," said Carlos.

"I think that would be kind of nice," said Nadia.

"But it could be dangerous," Lucy said.

"Can I try your glasses on?" asked Darma. But wearing Emiko's glasses only made things blurry and gave Darma a headache.

When Ms. Plum asked Emiko to go to the closet for more pink paper for making valentines, everyone knew Emiko would get a cute animal.

"Something soft and fuzzy," Jeremy predicted.

"A pretty one," agreed Jovi.

"A bunny."

"A puppy."

"A-a-an alligator?" said Brad.

Because that's what Emiko brought out of the closet. A very cross-looking alligator straining at a leash made of rope.

"Isn't he darling!" cried Emiko.

"Tell me, since when is a scaly old alligator darling?"

"Alligator?" said Emiko. "What alligator?"

"Uh, there. On that leash in your hand," Eric pointed out.

Emiko looked down. "You mean my poodle?"

"Poodle!" Mindy threw up her hands. "You think that's a poodle?"

Emiko smiled happily. "I've always wanted a poodle just like this, with fluffy white fur and a pink, sparkly collar. Oh, look, he wants to be petted."

The alligator lurched toward Brad's foot, snapping his jaws viciously.

Brad jumped back just in time.

The gator turned and hurtled himself at Tashala, who scrambled atop her desk chair a hair ahead of his jaws.

"Look, he wants to play," cried Emiko. "Here, Bubbles. That's a good Bubbles. Yes, you are a good doggy. Mmmm. Mmm. Mmm."

Emiko bent down and urged the alligator toward her with little kissy sounds.

"Watch out," said Carlos. "He'll bite your nose off!"

But before the alligator reached her, he lunged at Eric's hand. Eric scrambled onto his chair, too.

Emiko giggled, as if Bubbles had done something sweet.

"Come on, Bubbles. Let's go for a walk," Emiko said. Then she looked at Ms. Plum. "Can I show him around?"

Ms. Plum, who was intently working on her valentines for the class party, glanced up

and nodded. She seemed surprised to see several kids on top of their chairs.

"Class, let's the rest of you focus on your art project."

With a tug on his rope, Emiko pulled Bubbles toward the back of the room. The alligator seemed unhappy to leave all those ankles and toes, but soon he caught a whiff of Clyde, the hamster. He lunged at the table by the window, clawing at the table leg, trying to reach the helpless animals on top.

Hip-Hop quickly opened his eyes. Clyde scampered in terrified circles around his cage.

"Emiko, make Bubbles stop! Can't you see what he's doing?" said Mindy.

"Can't you see what he is?" asked Lucy.

Emiko seemed confused by the questions. For the first time ever, she looked a little hurt. "I don't see why everyone's being so mean about Bubbles."

"He's a dangerous animal!" said Lucy.

With that, Emiko burst out laughing. "You guys are such jokers. Come on, Bubbles, let's go back to our desk and work on our valentines."

The alligator followed Emiko, his slit eyes glaring, his tail lashing back and forth.

Everyone in the front row quickly pulled their feet back.

But Jeremy was too slow. Suddenly Bubbles's jaws locked onto the hem of Jeremy's blue jeans, and the alligator began to pull him from his chair!

"Alligators drag their prey into the water to drown them," observed Carlos.

"Emiko! Stop him!" cried Nadia.

"He's just playing. What is everybody's problem?"

"Help!" cried Jeremy, who was jumping about, trying to throw off Bubbles.

"Emiko! Look!"

Bubbles had stopped pulling and now had his claws sunk into Jeremy's pant leg. He looked up at Jeremy with a nasty grin on his face.

"Help!" Jeremy swung at him wildly, afraid to get any fingers too close. "Help!"

The whole class screamed at Emiko. "Do something!"

Emiko hesitated, then pulled off her glasses and peered at Bubbles.

Her face dropped. Her eyes widened. Her hand flew to her mouth in astonishment.

"Bubbles, stop!" she commanded. "Get down right now!"

Bubbles glanced over at her.

She stamped her foot. "Now!"

Bubbles grumbled, but then he released Jeremy's pant leg.

Emiko grabbed his leash. She squinted at the rope for a moment.

"I thought this was pink with sparkles," she said sadly.

Emiko led Bubbles back toward the closet.

"I thought you were a poodle. I've always wanted a poodle."

Bubbles made a casual swipe of a claw toward Becky Oh's foot. Emiko frowned.

"You're not a poodle at all," she concluded, scooting him into the closet and closing the door.

She turned back toward the class.

"Sorry," she said. "I guess he really was an alligator."

"Yes," was the general agreement. What a relief! At last Emiko saw the world as it really was.

"Just an alligator," Emiko sighed, heading back toward her desk. She sat down. She cleaned off her glasses. She looked over at Hip-Hop, the toad, and frowned sadly. Then slowly, slowly, she began to smile.

"But wasn't he the cutest little alligator you ever saw!" she suddenly said.

"Emiko!" cried Becky Oh. "No!"

"Well, he was. Did you see how adorable his green eyes were? And I think he was very smart. You could just tell by his expression."

The whole class groaned.

Ms. Plum didn't say anything. She held up the valentine she had just made. It seemed to have more glue than glitter, but Ms. Plum smiled happily and started her next valentine.

ϱϱϱϱϱϱ

"What is Ms. Plum?" asked Eric one windy March day at lunch.

Most of the kids from Ms. Plum's class sat together in the cafeteria. There was just so much to talk about and no one else to talk about it with. If they kept their voices low, they found they could speak out loud to each other about what really happened in Ms. Plum's class.

"Ms. Plum is our teacher. Duh," said Brad.

"Yeah, but is she like a witch? I mean, how can she do those things?"

"She would have to be a good witch," said Darma.

"I think she's a magic fairy," said Emiko.

"Maybe it's the closet that's magic," said Carlos. "Maybe it's not Ms. Plum at all."

"Nah, I think Ms. Plum is the magic," said Brad.

He sounded so certain that Carlos suddenly wondered how Brad could be so sure. Had Brad had some sort of magic experience?

"I bet if some other teacher got that room, it would just be a regular old closet," Tashala said.

"Hey, what do you think would happen if Ms. Plum went in the closet herself?" said Becky Oh. "Have you noticed, she never gets anything for herself."

"Would she get an animal?" asked Nadia.

"I know," said Eric. "Next time she asks for something, nobody raise your hand. Then she'll have to go in herself."

Everyone liked this idea, except Carlos. But he was outnumbered and had to go along with the plan.

"Remember," said Eric. "No one raises their hand."

ᲒᲒᲒᲒᲒᲒ

Chapter Nine

Birds of a Feather

"Who can get me a box of pushpins?" asked Ms. Plum a few days later.

Not a student raised a hand.

Ms. Plum looked surprised. She glanced over at Carlos.

Carlos clasped his hands together in front of him and held on tight. He pretended to be interested in something on his thumb.

"Well, I, uh . . ." Ms. Plum stood uncertainly. "I guess I'll have to get them myself."

She gave the class one more puzzled glance, then stepped into the closet.

In a moment she was back out, a box of plum-colored pushpins in her hand.

For a second it looked like nothing else had come out with her. ("Of course," whispered Darma, "because she's perfect.") But then a small peacock came bobbing out. It followed her to the front of the room.

Its tail feathers were down, drab and dragging along the floor. It didn't look very smart either.

"I expected like a tiger," whispered Tashala.

"Or a unicorn," Emiko whispered back.

"Now, class, let's get back to our science lesson."

Ms. Plum had set up an experiment on sound. Twenty water glasses sat across a table—each one filled with a little more water than the last.

She began to tap each glass with a metal spoon.

"Notice the different sounds."

"Ooooooooh," breathed the class in awe.

Ms. Plum smiled, then noticed that everyone had their eyes on something behind her.

Ms. Plum turned around. She had the distinct impression that the peacock had just snapped its tail feathers shut behind her.

She turned back to the class and began pinging on the glasses, going up the musical scale. This time, just as the class began to ooh and aah, she whirled around.

"Aha!" she cried.

The peacock's tail was spread into a glorious fan of luminous blues and greens and golds.

The bird quickly shut its tail and pecked at the floor, not meeting Ms. Plum's eye. Slowly it wandered away.

"Now then," Ms. Plum said. "Who can tell me why each glass sounds different?"

"Ahhhhhhhhhh!" cried the class.

Ms. Plum frowned and glanced over at the peacock. Clearly, it was just shutting its tail, pretending it hadn't been showing off.

"Now, class, please note this for your scientific pleasure," Ms. Plum said.

As she tapped each glass, the water turned a different color.

"Awesome," cried Carlos. The rest of the class chimed agreement.

Ms. Plum looked up, beaming.

But everyone was looking into the corner behind her.

She didn't bother to whirl around. She knew all she would see was the peacock closing its tail and acting like it didn't know anything.

"All right, if that's the way you want it," she said darkly.

She tapped each glass, and a different flower blossomed above the water.

The kids murmured their amazement.

The peacock snapped open its tail. It looked like an American flag.

The kids gasped.

Ms. Plum wafted her spoon above the flowers, and each flower sounded like a different instrument.

"Wow!" said the kids.

The peacock snapped open its tail.

"Amazing!" the class shouted as stars appeared to twinkle up and down its plumage.

Ms. Plum played "Mary Had a Little Lamb" with the glasses and flowers.

The peacock opened its tail. It looked like a garden of jewels.

Ms. Plum played "The Star-Spangled Banner."

The peacock opened its tail. Miniature fireworks erupted all over it.

The entire class stood up and gave the peacock a standing ovation, stamping their feet and whistling.

Ms. Plum set down her spoon.

"Come along, please," she said firmly to the bird.

She shooed it back into the closet and shut the door.

Then she marched back up to her desk and picked up her spoon.

Darma hesitated, then raised her hand.

"Yes, Darma." Ms. Plum looked rather cross.

Darma took a deep breath. "Well, uh, why did you get a peacock?"

"I guess he just happened to wander out," Ms. Plum said with a curious look at the closet. "I'm very sorry he distracted you all so horribly."

"Oh, he wasn't distracting. He was beautiful," said Mindy.

"Super," "Awesome," "Fantastic," "Unbelievable," echoed the other kids.

"Yes, I suppose he was," Ms. Plum said. "It's perfectly understandable that you would rather see him." Her lip trembled just a bit.

The kids nodded and agreed they'd never seen anything so grand.

Ms. Plum said, "Oh," and turned back to her lineup of glasses. She began to pull the flowers from the water.

"So, I guess that's enough science for today," she said, sounding a little sad.

The kids glanced at each other.

Darma raised her hand.

"Yes, Darma," said Ms. Plum.

"Please, don't stop," she said. "We want to see it."

Every student nodded his or her head.

"Please!" cried Mindy.

"Please!" said Nadia.

Even Carlos said, "Please, Ms. Plum. Your demonstrations are the best."

"Really?" said Ms. Plum.

"Totally," said Brad.

"Well, I suppose we do have some time."

The class clapped and smiled, and Brad gave a piercing two-fingered whistle.

Ms. Plum straightened her plum-colored skirt, smoothed down her hair, and pushed her sparkly glasses a little higher up her nose.

She smiled, then said quietly, "Thank you, class."

Then, like a famous conductor, Ms. Plum raised her spoon over the glasses and flowers and proceeded to play Beethoven's world-famous "Ode to Joy."

Chapter Ten
Shadows

One day in April, while Carlos snooped around the empty classroom during lunch recess, he opened the door to the closet and slipped inside. Being supersmart, he wondered why he hadn't thought of this before.

Carlos smelled the mysterious smell. He looked at all the colored pencils and glue sticks. He took a red licorice stick from the big jar on the shelf. He was just about to take a bite when he heard a faint rustle. He looked around, but there wasn't anything there. Even so, it felt like something was watching him from the dark. He decided he better leave.

Stuffing the licorice in his pocket, Carlos sneaked out of the closet and shut the door.

Just then Eric came into the classroom. "What's that?" he said.

"What's what?" said Carlos, his heart beating fast.

"You've been in the closet," said Eric.

"Have not," said Carlos. How could Eric tell?

"Where'd that wolf come from, then?" said Eric.

"What wolf?"

"Right there," said Eric, pointing at Carlos's heel. "Right behind you."

Carlos whirled around, but there wasn't anything there.

"Now he's behind your leg. He turned when you did," said Eric.

"You're just making that up," said Carlos, twisting around. He couldn't see anything.

Just then Mindy came in. Her eyes widened.

"You've been in the closet, haven't you?" She pointed toward Carlos's heel.

"Have not!" cried Carlos.

But it was no use, because everyone could see the little wolf. Everyone except Carlos. No matter how fast he turned, the wolf turned faster, so he was always out of sight behind Carlos.

"What's he look like?" Carlos asked.

"Like he would eat a passel of baby chickens," said Tashala.

"Scraggly and mean," said Becky Oh.

"His teeth are really long," Nadia added nervously.

"I think he's kind of cute," said Emiko.

Carlos ran to the mirror. But still he couldn't see it.

"He moves whenever you do. Like he's hooked to you or something," said Brad.

"It's not true!" said Carlos, swallowing back the lump in his throat.

Then Ms. Plum came in. Carlos felt his heart jump like there was a squirrel inside his chest. What would happen when she found out he'd gone into the supply closet without permission?

But Ms. Plum didn't seem to notice the wolf.

And even though every kid in Ms. Plum's room knew Carlos had sneaked into the supply closet, no one told on him. They went over their spelling words as if it were just a regular afternoon.

Ms. Plum asked Carlos to come to the blackboard to write out their first spelling word: *kleptomaniac*.

"Someone who can't stop stealing things,"

announced Becky Oh. She liked the especially hard words Ms. Plum sometimes gave. They were always interesting.

Carlos stood to go to the board. That's when he saw the wolf reflected in the window glass.

It was thin, low-slung, like a giant rat. And it followed him up to the chalkboard.

Now he could feel its warm breath, sensed it nearly touching him with its long, sharp nose. He hurried up to the blackboard, wrote out the word, and hurried back to his desk.

Ms. Plum announced their next word. "Jealousy."

Carlos didn't hear it. All he could feel was the presence of the wolf at his heel. He felt like the wolf might bite him on the back of his ankle, and he wanted to rub his ankle, but he was afraid he would touch the wolf.

When the bell rang, Carlos sat at his desk, waiting. All the kids glanced at him as they went out the door. Carlos didn't look at them.

Finally, when they were all gone, Carlos went up to Ms. Plum's desk.

"Can I take him back, Ms. Plum? Please?" he whispered.

"Take what back, dear?" said Ms. Plum, looking up from the work sheets she was grading.

"The wolf."

"Wolf?"

"Can't you see it?" Carlos waved toward his heel.

Ms. Plum stood up, leaned over her desk, and squinted.

"I don't see anything, Carlos," she said.

Carlos hung his head.

"I went in the closet," he said. "Without permission. I took some licorice."

Carlos set the limp red vine on her desk. "And then *he* came out," Carlos added, nodding toward his heel.

"Oh, I see."

"Can I take him back? Please, Ms. Plum."

"Yes, I think that would be the smart thing to do."

Carlos hurried into the closet and back out again.

"Do you see him, Ms. Plum?" he asked.

"No."

"You sure?"

Ms. Plum nodded.

"But you never could see him," Carlos pointed out.

"True. But what do you think?" said Ms. Plum. "Is he still there?"

Carlos knew he was gone. He could feel it inside.

"I'm glad you couldn't see him. He was really creepy," Carlos said. "Why couldn't you see him?"

"Maybe because that's not what I see when I look at you," Ms. Plum said.

Carlos was almost afraid to ask, but he did. "What do you see?"

"I see someone very special who will learn and grow all his life," said Ms. Plum with a smile.

"That doesn't sound so special," Carlos said quietly.

"Oh, but it is," said Ms. Plum. "You'll see soon enough."

After a moment, Carlos asked, "Does this mean I'll never get a chance at the closet?"

"There's always another chance at the closet for everyone," she said firmly.

Then Ms. Plum handed Carlos one of her plums. It was plump and purple and shimmered as if covered with a silvery dust. Ms. Plum didn't give out her plums very often.

As Carlos hurried across the schoolyard, he bit into his plum. It filled his mouth with springtime, earth, and honey.

He took another bite. He could feel the prickle of grass and the lazy heat of a summer afternoon. He took another bite. Autumn leaves crackled and popped, tickling his mouth. He took his last bite. He could taste frost sparkles and the blue shadows of snow.

It was the most amazing thing he had ever eaten.

Carlos grinned and ran for his school bus. It was still there! It was as if the bus and all the kids inside were waiting just for him.

Chapter Eleven

The Weight of the World

When Becky Oh squinched up her eyes and put her hand on her hip, she could scold a wall if she wanted to. "Why do you have to stand there so still and flat?" she would complain.

"Stop being so hard," she'd tell the floor.

"You're always wet," she'd grumble to water.

Becky could complain about just about anything. Today she was mumbling and grumbling because she thought Ms. Plum was being really boring. They were learning about grammar—nouns and verbs and adjectives. Becky usually liked words, but the day was boiling hot and Becky's head felt heavy and dull. When Ms. Plum underlined the nouns in the sentence on the board, the chalk made a horrible squeak and broke in two.

"Becky, dear, could you please get me a new piece of chalk?" she asked.

Becky scowled. She could even complain about being picked for the closet!

She tromped up to the closet and slipped inside.

It was much cooler in there. And she could smell erasers and . . . lemon drops? She stood there for a long time, until she heard Ms. Plum calling.

"Becky, please, hurry up." Even Ms. Plum seemed a little crabby today.

Becky grabbed a stick of chalk, then heard a tiny "hee-haw." She looked down. There at her feet was a little donkey, about the size of a squirrel. His coat was a soft gray. His eyes were bright. Strapped to his sides were two big yellow baskets that looked perfect for carrying things.

Becky tucked the chalk into one of the baskets and walked slowly from the closet. She didn't want Ms. Plum to think she would hurry just because Ms. Plum had told her to.

The donkey carried the chalk to Ms. Plum and stood there while she bent down and took the chalk out of the basket. "Thank you, dear," said Ms. Plum.

Then the donkey trotted after Becky to her desk.

Ms. Plum began to drone on again. Becky saw Tashala sigh and lay her head in her arms.

Becky scribbled out a note:

Ms. Plum is so B-O-R-I-N-G!

She put it in one of the donkey's baskets, and he seemed to know right where to take it. He trotted over to Tashala and gave her a little nudge with his velvety nose. Tashala looked at Becky's note, then scribbled out one in return:

It's too hot for nouns.

The donkey trotted back to Becky, frisking his long ears and glancing up at her as he delivered the note.

Becky wrote out another note:

It's not fair. Ms. Plum should give us extra recess.

Mindy saw the note over Becky's shoulder, and she quickly wrote her own note:

I hat grammar and speling.

She stuffed it into the donkey's basket along with Becky's note.

Lucy saw what was going on and wrote her own note:

Ms. Plum shouldn't use chalk. It squeaks and is dusty, which could be dangerous to your health.

Everyone began to write their own mean notes because it was hot and Ms. Plum was making them work too hard and the sun was too bright and the sky was too blue and the room suddenly had a funny, new smell.

The little donkey clip-clopped patiently from desk to desk as everyone crammed notes into his baskets.

Ms. Plum was too busy writing on the board to notice the donkey going from desk to desk. She was flushed and had a streak of chalk across her cheek.

The donkey got slower and slower with each note. The notes seemed awfully heavy for him. By the time he picked up Jovi's note, the little donkey's legs were trembling with the weight.

When the donkey limped past Becky, she noticed there was sweat crisscrossing his back where the straps for the baskets lay. His tiny head was bent low. He was working hard, and he didn't look up at her with his once bright eyes.

Becky swallowed.

"Wait," she whispered.

The little donkey stopped.

Becky hesitated, then reached down.

"I think I'll take out my note," she said.

Mindy looked at Becky, then reached down and took out her note, too.

Eric did it next, and then so did most of the other kids.

By the time the donkey got to Ms. Plum, he was frisking his ears and his eyes were shining and there was only one note left in the basket.

Ms. Plum put down her chalk and lifted out the note.

She read it out loud:

I am liking to learn nouns. Thank you, Ms. Plum. Jovi.

Ms. Plum blinked. She pushed her sparkly glasses back up her sticky, hot nose.

"Why, thank you, Jovi," she said. "I like teaching you nouns."

She smiled at the class.

"Still, it is awfully hot, don't you think?"

Becky raised her hand. "Maybe we could go out on the lawn and sit under the tree. It would be nice and cool in the shade."

"What an excellent idea," said Ms. Plum. "Class, let's go do that."

"Cool idea!" said Jeremy. "Get it—cool?"

"Hooray for Becky Oh," said Emiko.

"Go Becky Oh!" said Jeremy.

And Becky grinned shyly because suddenly everyone was cheering her name, and she couldn't think of a thing wrong with that.

Chapter Twelve

The Purr-fect Place

Nadia worried. A lot. She didn't want to worry, but every morning, first thing, Lucy told her all the bad things Lucy's dad saw on the news.

"The ice caps are melting!" Lucy told Nadia. "There are angry cows running around. And birds are getting this really bad flu.

"The world is a mess. It's getting messier every day!" said Lucy, shaking her head the way her dad did every night.

Every day Lucy had lots of new things for Nadia to worry about.

"If you get bitten by a rabid weasel, you have to get fourteen shots," she said. "If you look straight at a rhinoceros, it will definitely attack."

"Can't I worry about stuff when I'm a grown-up?" asked Nadia.

"Don't you get it?" cried Lucy. "You probably won't even live to be a teenager!"

So Nadia bit her fingernails until they were ragged stubs. She had dark smudges under her eyes because she couldn't sleep. If someone dropped a book on the floor, Nadia ducked.

"Who'd like to get me some purple paper?" asked Ms. Plum.

Of course, Lucy waved her hand super hard because purple was her favorite color, but Ms. Plum picked Nadia.

Nadia jumped up. She had wanted Ms. Plum to call on her all year.

"Remember the scary falcon and the nasty wolf," whispered Lucy.

"Oh." Nadia stopped, then said, "Ms. Plum? Maybe Lucy should do it."

"I asked you, Nadia," said Ms. Plum.

She didn't say it in a mean way, but even so, Nadia knew it meant that she had to go into the closet. So she walked over, clenched her hands by her sides, and stepped inside.

There were no falcons or wolves or scary things anywhere. Only a smell like the woods in summer, and wonderful things beckoning from every shelf.

Nadia picked up three sheets of purple paper, then heard a soft purring sound.

There on the shelf next to the paper sat a little striped cat, its coat gleaming softly. It leapt gracefully onto Nadia's shoulder and curled up there beside her ear.

"Look," said Nadia, stepping shyly from the closet. "Look!"

Everyone oohed and aahed, even the boys, because Nadia's little cat was just perfect.

Nadia hadn't known she wanted a cat until she got this one. How soft it was. How pretty its striped fur and its pink nose. How calm its dark yellow eyes.

"Thank you, Nadia," said Ms. Plum after everyone had gotten a good look at the little cat.

As Nadia headed back to her desk, Ms. Plum picked up her book to continue the story she was reading to the class.

"'The barn was very large. It was very old,'" she read.

"Cats carry tons of diseases," whispered Lucy when Nadia sat down at her desk.

"Really?" Nadia shifted her shoulders uneasily.

The little cat snuggled against her neck, soft and warm.

"I think I'll give it some of my tuna sandwich," Nadia whispered.

"Tuna fish has some kind of worm thing," said Lucy. "It gets into your bones, I think, and eats them up."

"Oh." Nadia frowned.

The tiny cat purred against her ear.

"Plus there's this weird algae thing happening in the ocean," Lucy hissed, glancing to see if Ms. Plum was listening.

"'It smelled of grain and of harness dressing and of axle grease and of rubber boots . . . ,'" Ms. Plum was still reading.

"And that probably means that soon there won't be enough oxygen in the air anymore," said Lucy.

"Right." Nadia's shoulders slumped. The cat snuggled against her neck, soft and warm.

"You better give me your cat," Lucy said. "It could bite you, you know."

Nadia reached up and lifted the cat from her shoulder. She held it in her hand. The cat opened its mouth. It did have sharp white teeth. Then it licked Nadia's finger with its pink tongue. Its tongue was soft and scratchy at the same time.

"Plus a giant meteor could hit the earth," said Lucy. "That's a real fact!"

Nadia ran her finger along the back of her cat. Its fur rippled under her finger like a piece of velvet.

"Elephants are most likely to attack at dawn," said Lucy.

The cat leapt back onto Nadia's shoulder and snuggled down again. It purred so loudly that Nadia had a hard time hearing Lucy.

"You can lose your hearing if you listen to really loud music," said Lucy.

"Hmmmm," said Nadia.

"Are you listening?" said Lucy as loud as she dared.

Nadia nodded dreamily. But she wasn't really listening. All she could hear was the cat's deep, contented purr. It was like soft, faraway thunder. And Nadia remembered she liked the rain.

She looked out the window. It was nearly summer. The tree outside Ms. Plum's window was green with leaves that shifted with shadows and sunlight. A sparrow scolded and bobbed on one of the twigs. A tiny silvery plane whispered across the soft blue sky.

On the table by the window, Clyde, the hamster, nibbled on a sunflower seed, his

whiskers quivering. Hip-Hop blinked in the sun.

Ms. Plum closed her book. She placed it on her desk with the vase of plum flowers and jar of plum-colored pencils and the basket of plums dusted with silver.

She tilted her head, and her glasses sparkled in the sunlight. She smiled.

Everyone smiled back.

"What a wonderful class you are. What a wonderful year," said Ms. Plum.

Nadia nodded. Everyone nodded. Ms. Plum really did have the best class in all of Springtime Elementary.

And Nadia was glad she was there.

ϱϱϱϱϱϱ

Ms. Plum gazed out the window of her empty classroom. The playground was empty. The halls were empty. School was out for the summer.

Ms. Plum sighed. Then she did something she did every year. She walked down the aisles and touched each desk as she passed, remembering each and every student. She dabbed at her eye and snuffled just a little bit.

Surely this was her best class ever.

Scooping up the plum-colored pencils on her desk, she went to the closet and set them in a pencil basket on the shelf.

She stared into the very back of the back of the closet, where the dark was as soft and as deep as velvet.

"My best class ever," she said, pushing up her sparkly glasses.

Then, after a moment, she said, "You're right. I do say that every year, don't I?"

PLUM

She left the closet, then suddenly turned and declared loudly into the closet, "And every year it's true!"

Then she closed the closet door for the summer.

About the Author

Bonny Becker is the author of a dozen children's books, including the *New York Times* bestseller *A Visitor for Bear*. The idea for Ms. Plum originated in Bonny's childhood love of books with magical helpers such as Mary Poppins and Mrs. Piggle-Wiggle. As a kid, Bonny was most like Carlos, the straight-A student in Ms. Plum's class who feels frustrated that being book-smart isn't getting him everything he wants. Like Carlos, Bonny says she's learned that many other things, like courage, kindness, and humor, are just as important in life.

Bonny hopes kids who read this book will feel less afraid of making mistakes, and will see that stumbles are a part of how everyone grows and figures things out.

Bonny and her husband live in Seattle, Washington. Visit her website at bonnybecker.com.